FOLLOW THE SWALLOW

Julia Donaldson

Illustrated by

Martin Ursell

EGMONT

We bring stories to life

Book Band: Purple

Lexile® measure: 480L

First published in Great Britain 2000
This Reading Ladder edition published 2016
by Egmont UK Limited
The Yellow Building, 1 Nicholas Road, London W11 4AN
Text copyright © Julia Donaldson 2000
Illustrations © Martin Ursell 2000
The author and illustrator have asserted their moral rights
ISBN 978 1 4052 8200 0
www.egmont.co.uk
A CIP catalogue record for this title is available from the British Library.
Printed in Singapore
26851/027

Egmont takes its responsibility to the planet and its inhabitants very seriously.
All the papers we use are from well-managed forests run by responsible suppliers.

Series consultant: Nikki Gamble

FOLLOW THE
SWALLOW

Julia Donaldson

Illustrated by

Martin Ursell

For Helen
J.D.

For Anne
M.U.

Chack the blackbird was learning to fly.

So was Apollo the swallow.

That was how they met.

'Who are you?' asked Chack.

'I'm Apollo. I'm a swallow.'

'And what do you swallow?'

'Flies, mostly,' said Apollo. 'And who are you?'

'I'm Chack. I'm a blackbird.'

'You look brown to me,' said Apollo.

'I may be brown now but one day I'll

be black,' said Chack.

'I don't believe you!' said Apollo.

Apollo showed Chack his nest. It was

on a cobwebby shelf in a shed.

'I won't always live here,' he said.

'One day I'll fly away to Africa.'

'I don't believe you!' said Chack.

Chack showed Apollo his nest.

It was in a tree covered in white blossom.

'One day the tree will be covered in tasty orange berries,' said Chack.

'I don't believe you!' said Apollo.

The days grew longer and warmer.
Apollo started going around with a lot
of other swallows. They kept gathering
on the roof of the shed and then flying
off all together.

'What are you doing?' asked Chack.

'Practising flying to Africa!' said Apollo.

'I don't believe you!' said Chack.

The white blossom fell off Chack's tree

and some little green berries appeared.

'They'll be orange one day,' he told Apollo.

'I don't believe you!'

said Apollo.

Slowly the berries on the tree grew bigger and changed colour, from green . . . to yellow . . . and at last to orange.

'Now Apollo will believe me!' said Chack. He flew to the shed to tell his friend about the orange berries.

'Come to the tree! Come to the tree!' he called.

I can't wait to show Apollo!

But Apollo had gone! He and the other swallows had just set off for Africa.

Chack flew after the swallows. He flew
and he flew till he reached the sea.
There he met a jumpy dolphin.

'Can you take a message to Apollo the swallow from Chack the blackbird?' asked Chack. 'He's on his way to Africa.'

'What is the message?' asked the dolphin.

'Come to the tree!' said Chack, and he

flew back to eat some of the tasty orange

berries.

The jumpy dolphin swam and leapt and
dived.

It took him a long time to reach Africa.

There he met a grumpy camel.

'Can you take a message to Apollo
the swallow from Chack the blackbird?'
asked the dolphin.

'What's the message?' asked the camel.

'Er . . . er . . . "Jump in the sea!"' said
the dolphin.

The grumpy camel trudged slowly across the desert . . .

. . . till he reached a wide river. There he
met a greedy crocodile.

'Can you take a message to Apollo the
swallow from Chack the blackbird?'
asked the camel.

'What's the message?' asked the
crocodile.

'Er . . . er . . . "Grumpy like me!"' said
the camel.

The greedy crocodile took his time

swimming and snapping his way down

the river . . .

. . . till he came to a forest. There he met

a playful monkey.

'Can you take a message to Apollo

the swallow from Chack the blackbird?'

asked the crocodile.

Monkey
for tea

'What is the message?' asked the monkey.

'Er. . . er. . . "Monkey for tea!"' said the crocodile.

The playful monkey swung from branch

to branch till he came to a fig tree . . .

On the ground lay a lot of rotten figs.

Feeding on the rotten figs were a lot of

fruitflies, and snapping at the fruitflies

were a lot of swallows.

'I've got a message for Apollo the swallow,' said the monkey.

'That's me!' said one of the swallows.

'What is the message and who is it from?'

'It's from Chack the blackbird and the message is . . . er, er, "One, two, three, whee!"' said the monkey.

'One, two, three, whee!' said Apollo.

'That's a funny message! Well, I've been
in Africa for half a year now. It's time for
me to fly back to the garden. I can find
out what Chack means.'

Apollo and the other swallows flew back,

over the forest . . .

and the river . . .

and the desert . . .

and the sea . . .

. . . till they reached the garden. Apollo
flew to Chack's tree. It was covered in
white blossom.

A big blackbird flew down from the tree.

'I'm looking for my friend Chack,' said
Apollo.

'That's me!' said Chack.

'I don't believe you!'

said Apollo.

'You're black and Chack was brown.'

'I'm Chack as sure as eggs are eggs,'
said Chack. 'And talking of eggs, I've
got something to show you.'

He flew up to a nest in the tree. Apollo
flew after him. A brown bird was sitting
in the nest.

'Time for your worm-break, Rowena,'
said Chack.

The brown bird flew off, and there in the nest Apollo saw some pale, bluey-green eggs. He counted them . . . 'One, two, three. So the message wasn't "One, two, three, whee!" It was "One, two, three eggs!"' he said.

'No, it wasn't!' said Chack. 'It was

"Come to the tree!"'

'Well, I have come to the tree and I've

seen the eggs, and I think they're

beautiful,' said Apollo.

The message was "Come to the tree!"

'But the message wasn't about the eggs,

it was about the orange berries,' said Chack.

'Orange berries! Orange berries! You're

not still on about orange berries, are you?'

Apollo started to laugh.

'But there really were orange berries!'
said Chack. 'There were and there will
be again.'

Apollo thought hard.

'All right, then,' he said, ' I believe you.'

Did you spot these animals?

Ostrich

Colobus

Leopard

Fennec Fox

Okapi

Bongo

Hornbill

Giraffe

Hartebeest

White Rhinoceros

Potto

Lioness

Zebra

Kudu

Lechwe

Thompson's Gazelle

Goldfinch

Mandrill

African Elephant

Blue Tit

Badger

Bushbuck

Vulture

Cape Buffalo

Hereford Cow

Greenfinch